THIS CANDLEWICK BOOK BELONGS TO:

_____

_____

_____

_____

For Charles

Copyright © 1992 by Camilla Ashforth

First U.S. paperback edition 1995
First published in Great Britain in 1992 by Walker Books Ltd., London.

Library of Congress Cataloging-in-Publication Data
Ashforth, Camilla.
Monkey tricks / Camilla Ashforth.—1st U.S. ed.
"First published in Great Britain in 1992 by Walker Books Ltd., London"—T.p. verso.
Summary: While his friend Horatio, a stuffed rabbit, enjoys the bungled
tricks of a mischievous monkey, James, a teddy bear wonders why
the monkey's props look so familiar.
ISBN 1-56402-170-X (hardcover)—ISBN 1-56402-454-7 (paperback)
[1. Toys—Fiction.   2. Behavior—Fiction.]   I. Title.
PZ7.A823Mo   1992   92-53013
[E]—dc20

2 4 6 8 10 9 7 5 3 1

Printed in Hong Kong

The pictures in this book were done in watercolor.

Candlewick Press
2067 Massachusetts Avenue
Cambridge, Massachusetts 02140

MONKEY TRICKS

by Camilla Ashforth

CANDLEWICK PRESS
CAMBRIDGE, MASSACHUSETTS

Horatio was practicing hopping.

HOP

HOP

HOP

WHOOPS!

He fell over a notice board.
"I'll ask James what this says,"
he thought.

James was looking in his Useful Box.
Someone had untidied it.
"What does this say?" asked Horatio.
"Johnny Conqueror Coming Today,"
said James. He looked worried.
"That naughty monkey!"

Horatio looked all around for
Johnny Conqueror.
"Jimmys and Jacks! Watch your backs!"
a voice called, and there was
Johnny Conqueror, pulling a wagon.

"I'm very good at juggling," he boasted.

He threw a string of beads into the air
and held out his hands to catch them.

But he missed and the beads
scattered everywhere.

Horatio clapped his hands.
"My beads look like this," thought
James, picking one up.

"For my next trick," shouted
Johnny Conqueror, "I take a long
piece of rope and knot it here
and twist it a little here . . ."

"That rope looks useful," thought James.
He looked in his Useful Box again.

Johnny Conqueror got into a tangle.
He needed James to untie him.
Horatio thought it was very funny.

"I'll show you how clever I am at balancing," said Johnny Conqueror, jumping onto a spool of thread! He stood on one leg and spun a dish above him.

The spool wobbled.

James looked worried.

"If that were my dish . . . ," he thought.

CRASH!

The spool spun away and
Johnny Conqueror fell over.
The dish broke.

"Oh, dear," thought James.
"Hooray!" shouted Horatio.

"To end the show," announced Johnny Conqueror, "I do my best trick. I disappear! All close your eyes and count to five."

"One ... two ... ," Horatio began.

"I know who untidied my Useful Box," whispered James.

"Three ... four ... ," added Horatio.

"And I'm going to catch him," James said.

"Five!" shouted Horatio and they opened their eyes.

Johnny Conqueror had disappeared.

"Fiddlesticks," said James. "He got away."

James began to clean up.

"Now I can show you my trick," said
Horatio, and he hopped for James.

James clapped his hands.

"That really is clever," he said, and
he gave Horatio a big hug.

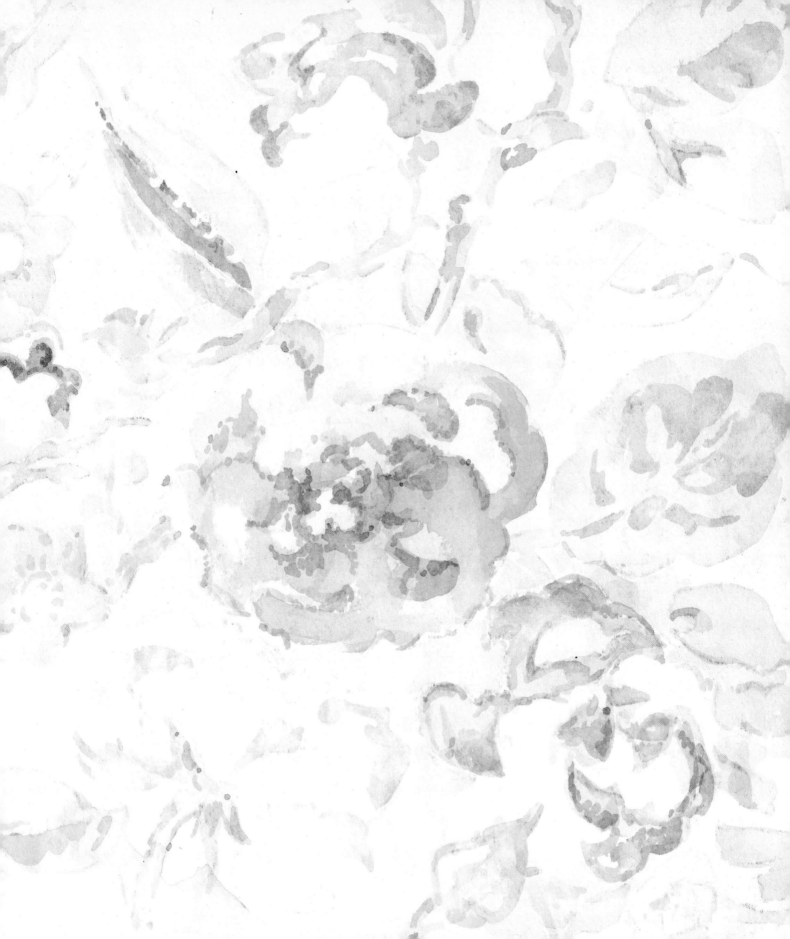

CAMILLA ASHFORTH's stories about James and Horatio—introduced
to readers in her first book, *Horatio's Bed*—were inspired
by the stuffed animals of her childhood. She based the character
of Johnny Conqueror on a stuffed monkey that used to be her brother's
favorite toy. "He's like a completely irrepressible, naughty little
boy who'll get away with things again and again," she says. "He'll
probably be pestering James and Horatio for a long time."